W9-BGS-572

ALL *of* US

Words by Kathryn Erskine • Pictures by Alexandra Boiger

PHILOMEL

PHILOMEL BOOKS
An imprint of Penguin Random House LLC, New York

First published in the United States of America by Philomel Books,
an imprint of Penguin Random House LLC, 2021

Visit us online at penguinrandomhouse.com.

Library of Congress Cataloging-in-Publication Data is available.

Manufactured in China

ISBN 9780593204696

1 3 5 7 9 10 8 6 4 2

Edited by Jill Santopolo • Design by Ellice M. Lee
Text set in LTC Cloister Oldstyle

The art was done with pencil and painted in Photoshop.

To family and friends—
yours and mine—
around the globe
—K. E.

To my family—here and there

A special thanks to
Justice Ruth Bader Ginsburg
for her lifelong fight for justice for all
—A. B.

Me . . .

can be we.

You . . .

can come, too.

They . . .

can be “Hey!”

It's all of us.

Hearts can unite.
Hands can set free.

Words can be heard.
We can all be.

ভালবাসা
DASHURI
upenzi
عشق
ALOHA
AMORE
jacayl
AŞK
LOVE
愛

Some pray out loud,

some close their eyes.

Some look to earth, some to the skies.

THEATER

Stars are so far,
worlds disappear.
Planets flung wide.
We all live here.

Mountains and streams,
deserts and towns . . .

Breathtaking sights . . .

Remarkable sounds.

Some build things up,
some create art.

Some help the earth,
some heal the heart.

Hands, hearts, and minds,
vibrant and strong.

Different, the same,
we all belong.

All kinds of kids,
thoughtful and free.
Sometimes in groups,

sometimes . . .

. . . just me.